The Hassassini

Russell Glashan

This book is a work of fiction. It is entirely the product of the author's imagination. Any resemblance to actual persons, living or dead, is purely coincidental.

Copyright © Russell Glashan 2024

* * *

The Hassassini.

Is an order that existed between 1090 and 1275 AD, founded by Hassan-i Sabbah. was a religious and military leader, founder of the Nizari Ismai'li sect, widely known as the *Hashshashin,* or the Order of Assassin. The modern term assassination is believed to stem from the tactics used by the Order of Assassins. Their preferred method of killing was by dagger, nerve poison, or arrows.

Today, the name Hassassini became the

modern version of assassins. The group is involved in the killings of their political enemies or those they deem a threat to their organisation. They resurrected their name from Hassan-i-Sabbah, and now call themselves…

With the fiery dragon as their symbol

The Hassassini.

Chapter One

Surveillance

Malcolm Bannister shivered. The late evening air was cooler than it had been in recent days. Summer was ending and the throes of autumn were beginning. The temperature had plummeted in the past few days, and Bannister wished he had brought a jumper with him.

By order of their boss, he and Pullman were on surveillance duty. He hated surveillance at the best and worst of times. Night time surveillance gave him the creeps. It was a feeling he never could shake off, especially on a black night and gloomy street such as this, all the way from his time as a rookie cop.

They parked up between two rows of drab Glasgow tenement buildings. Many of the windows were boarded up. They were being cleared for eventual demolition in the near future, or when the corporation could find the cash to do it. A few were still occupied. Within the year, Glasgow Corporation would complete a final clearance of the occupants and rehouse them. The down and outs who took over the empty flats would be kicked out to find somewhere else to go.

A stiff breeze pulled in the clouds, chilling the air even more. *'Please don't rain,'* he muttered to himself. He had been sitting here for hours with his partner, Bob Pullman. They were cold and hungry, with no real idea as to why they were here.

His boss, Superintendent Billy Monkhouse, told them precious little about the reason for tonight's watch. That in itself was unusual. More concerning, Monkhouse told them to, "look out for a female by the name of Isobel Cooper and trail her when she leaves the flat."

"Who is she, and what does she look like?" asked Bannister. "More to the point, what has she done?"

"She is slim, five foot two, with black longish hair," said his boss. "What she has done is for me to know and you to wonder for the time being. But…" Monkhouse hesitated, "Make sure she is safe."

"Boss, we are cops, not babysitters. You have to give us more to go on," said Bannister.

"That's all I can give you for now. Just do it."

"How long do we stay here?"

"Until she leaves the building." Without another word, Monkhouse walked away from the two men.

The poorly lit street was deserted, with only a few cars parked intermittently on both sides. At least half of the streetlights were gone, used as target practice by the local kids.

They parked up, then settled down to wait and watch. As sure as hell, the Glasgow weather didn't disappoint. It started to rain. Bannister sat as deep in the car as his bulk allowed in the cramped space of the unmarked blue Ford sedan. With his eyes permanently fixed on the third-floor window on the opposite side of the street, he shivered. "Brrrr." He wrapped his arms around his body as far as he could, trying to ward off the chill, wishing he had brought that pullover.

The passenger door opened with a jerk, and Bob Pullman thumped his backside into the seat. Bannister jumped, with his fist ready to smack the intruder hard on the face. He stopped in time as a giggling Pullman made himself comfortable.

"Fuck, man. You scared the bejesus out of me and almost got a bloody nose to the bargain," complained the big man.

His younger partner chuckled. "You're getting more nervous as you get older," he laughed as he chucked a pack of prepared sandwiches to his partner, bought from the local twenty-four-hour service station, "and here is a hot coffee to warm yer old bones," he said handing a plastic cup to the still fuming Bannister.

"Less of the old, if you don't mind. It's bloody freezing tonight," he remarked, "and my mind was elsewhere."

"On the job, I hope. Has anything happened?" He asked, glancing at the small ID picture they were watching for, sitting on the car dash. "Hmm, she is a looker, that's for sure."

Isobel Cooper's face was oval and pert, with green eyes and a slightly turned-up nose, with long black hair cascading down to the middle of her back. Bob nodded his approval.

"Nahh, Nothing," Bannister replied. "I'm not sure anything will happen. The flat has been in darkness since we arrived. All the lights in the place are out. I think we are in for a long, fruitless night, and a fucking cold one at that." He nodded, looking up at the window on the third floor on the other side of the street. "She has either gone to bed or gone out another way."

Isobel Cooper's face was oval and pert, with green eyes and a slightly turned-up nose, with long black hair cascading to the middle of her back. Bob nodded his approval. "Yep."

"Doubt it," replied Pullman. "The front door is the only way in or out. I checked earlier before we settled here."

"I know you did, but we can never be sure. If cooper clocked that we are on to her, she could have gone out a back window."

"I can't see that happening. She would have to be one hell of an athlete to scale down from that height. Besides, how should she guess we were on to her?" Pullman screwed his face as he answered the question. "There is also an eight-foot fence at the rear of the property, topped with rusted barbed wire."

"Yeah, I suppose you are right. I'm being paranoid because I don't know what this stake out is about, and I am bloody freezing." Bannister shivered. "The temperature has dropped in the past couple of hours, and it's going to rain again," he moaned.

"Malc, what's the story on this one? Why are we here?" Pullman asked.

"I have not got a clue. Monkhouse called me into his office and gave me that picture," he said, pointing to the picture on the car dash. "The boss told me to follow her if she leaves the building but wouldn't say why. Then we are to report her movements back to him without apprehending her," he sighed. "I hate being left in the dark with so little to go on."

Bannister yawned. Turning to his partner, he asked, "Bob, do you mind taking this watch? I am bushed. I ain't slept in almost forty-eight hours. This has been a double shift for me."

"Sure, no problem. I'll give you a shake if anything happens."

Bannister shuffled his six-foot four bulk into some kind of comfortable position to try to have a kip. The dark blue Ford Mondeo was not the most comfortable car to sleep in, especially if you are a six-foot four beefcake. He pulled his jacket close to his body, folded his arms around himself and attempted to rest awhile.

Pullman took up position, fixing his eyes on the window of the third-floor flat, hoping to God that he would see some action soon. He finished his crappy sandwich, sipped at his lukewarm coffee, sat back and waited.

In the almost four years Bannister and Pullman had been partners, the job in the force had involved them in many dozens of cases. Some had been dangerous, some gruesome. But hell, that's what being a cop was about. Both had gotten each other out of tricky escapes more than once. Bannister, who was the older of the two by nine years, was four years away from retirement.

Chapter Two

"Malcom," Bob Pullman shook his partner violently. "Action," he hissed.

Bannister struggled from his slumber with a jolt. He leaned forward as Pullman pointed up to the flat. A light had come on. "What's going on?" he asked, glancing at the clock on the dash. The time read four thirty-three. They had been here for over four hours. He rubbed his eyes. "What have you seen?"

"Not sure yet. Someone went through the front landing. At first, I thought it might be a neighbour. Then a couple of minutes later, a light came on inside the flat," Bob replied.

They both stared at the flat window. A curtain

moved. It shook from side to side as if someone brushed against it. "Something is happening at the window," Bannister acknowledged. "Hang fire for a few minutes. Let's see what materialises." He rolled down the window a few inches and listened. In the quietness of the deserted street, they heard a dull thud, and watched as a shadow appeared to fall to the floor. "Come on Bob. Let's get moving," called Bannister, hauling himself out of the Mondeo with Pullman following close behind.

As they reached the entrance to the flat, they heard footsteps coming down the stairs. "Shit. Who the hell puts a security panel on an auld building like this!" moaned an angry Bannister. As he struggled with the security panel, the intruder ran to the rear of the building. "Go get 'em, Bob," yelled the big cop as he ran up the three flights of stairs to the third floor, leaving Pullman to chase the running intruder.

Bannister stopped when he came to the door, which was slightly ajar. Putting his left hand against it, the black door moved easily to his touch. Pulling out his Glock 17 pistol, he took a deep breath and shouted. "Police! Stay where you are!" No sound came from the flat. He didn't expect any. He knew that he should wait for backup, or for his partner to return. However, the number of times he had broken that rule was countless. In any case, Pullman was busy chasing the other guy.

With no answer to his second shout, he shoved the door open a little more with his foot. As covert cops, both Bannister and Pullman were authorised to carry a small pistol. With two hands on the Glock, and the weapon aimed straight in front of him, he checked inside as far as he could see. Nothing. He pushed the door as wide as it could open, then he aimed his body at the wall in front of himself for cover. Swiftly, he shifted his position as he thumped his back against the other wall. Still, there was no response.

As he looked around the room, he saw nothing at first from his new vantage point. Then, edging himself along the wall with his back against it, he faced the open door in front of him on his lefthand side. Mentally, he ran through the rules of engagement. "Fuck it …armed police!" he roared as he threw himself to the left and into the final room.

"Oh, shit!" The scene in front of him almost made him throw up. He lowered his pistol and returned the weapon to the holster under his jacket. The body in front of him lay face down, with the head, or what was left of it, facing towards the kitchen door. The head had been battered to a pulp, brain and skull fragments peppered the beige carpet. Considering the severity of the beating, there was very little blood splatter.

Bannister called HQ. "We need backup and a forensic team. One dead." He gave the address over his mobile, without moving, as he stared at the dead body on the floor. The attacker had pulverised the face beyond recognition.

"Bannister!" the shout came from Pullman, who breathlessly made his way up the three flights of stairs. "Where are you? are you okay?"

"Yeah, yeah, I am fine, but the guy on the floor ain't. Watch your step. There's blood around."

Carefully, Pullman stepped into the flat and over to his partner's voice. Bannister was still leaning against the wall beside the body, taking in the scene before the paramedics arrived.

Pullman took one glimpse at the dead body's face and immediately turned his head away. "Oh, fuck," he said as he forced himself to look back at the scene. "Someone made sure she was gone."

"Yep." Bannister nodded grimly. "Your runner got away; I take it?"

"Yeah, it was too dark. He had a head start and vaulted over the high fence. Fit, whoever he was. I called for the dog squad, but I doubt it will do any good by the time they get here." Pullman had regained his breath. "The runner also wore a hoodie tied tight against the neck, so no visual either. Sorry boss."

"No worries. We will need a full team for this mess," Bannister said with a sigh.

"Any ideas on the body?" the body wore loose clothing, with the hood partially covering the now grotesque face. It would take ages for forensics to identify the dead guy, if at all.

Bannister shook his head. "Nahh, this is one for the mortuary guys to work out. Looks small though. Probably our girl," said Bannister. "I'd better inform the boss."

Bannister pulled his phone from his back pocket and dialled Monkhouse's private number. It was answered on the second ring. "Sir, we are inside the tenement. Not good news, I am afraid. We found a body." He waited for a reply.

It came after a noticeable gasp from Monkhouse. Bannister waited. After some minutes, "Was it the girl?"

"Sir, we don't know at this stage. We couldn't see the face. It is covered by a hood. We are leaving it to the crime lab guys first," he lied. "The body will be in the morgue within the hour. We will be there at eight in the morning to get Sour's results."

"Thanks, inspector, I will be there too." The phone clicked off without another word.

After the crime scene guys finished with their examination of the flat, they asked the paramedics to take the body to the mortuary. As they lifted the corpse into a black body bag, there was a dull thud on the floor. A mobile phone dropped from the body into the pool of still wet blood on the carpet.

Bannister looked over at his partner and nodded to the phone, indicating for Pullman to pick it up. The younger man glowered at the older man before he could say. *'Higher ranks prerogative.'*

Taking care not to step on any of the blood, he picked it up with two gloved fingers, trying not to feel squeamish, and deposited the bloody phone into an evidence bag being held open by a smiling Bannister.

Bannister examined the phone through the clear plastic bag for a few seconds before pressing the 'on' button. The screen remained blank. Hopefully, the battery only needs charging. "The geeks at the station will sort it out," he said.

"Come on mate. Let's get back to the station and fill in the first reports. Then we can have a break. By the way, you look like shit."

"Gee, thanks Bob. You're so full of compliments."

Chapter Three

The following morning, Bannister and Pullman, along with their boss, Billy Monkhouse, stood at the long glass window in the city morgue for a low-down on the body found at Isobel Cooper's flat.

"Good morning, Mr Saur," hailed Bannister to the pathologist.

Pullman acknowledged the white-coated man standing next to a stainless steel table with a nervous nod. Billy Monkhouse stood behind the two detectives, his hands clasped in front of him, with his inspector's cap held under his right arm. He stared motionless at the figure on the dissecting table. The deformed, grotesque head made it difficult for both detectives to look at it.

Monkhouse, however, stood straight to attention, impassive, as he continued to stare at the body. In front of the pathologist, the body was splayed out on the gleaming table, with the chest flaps wide open, revealing the deep red inners of blood and guts inside the empty cavity. Pullman wanted to throw up, but wiped the corners of his mouth with a clean white handkerchief. A white modesty sheet covered the private parts across the thighs of the figure on the stainless steel table.

Pullman did not like this guy, pathologist Peter Saur. He made him shiver. The pathologist stood over six-foot-four inches tall and skinny. His long narrow face drawn in at the cheeks, exposing the sharpness of his cheekbones. His long bony fingers revealed the thick lines of his veins, and his hands constantly moved, as if they wanted to be always touching something. Pullman thought he had a 'Frankenstein' look about him and deader than the dead he examined.

"Good morning, gentlemen," Saur acknowledged to the three men in a deep Germanic accent which echoed through the mortuary. He began to announce his findings. "Your victim is male, five-foot-eleven inches tall. He is approximately twenty-nine-years' old, and he was a very fit individual before his demise…"

"Did you say male?" interrupted a surprised Bannister.

Behind him, Billy Monkhouse suppressed a smile with a deep intake of breath. The body was not female. It was not Isobel Cooper. He replaced his cap and left without a word to his two detectives.

Peter Saur was annoyed at being interrupted. He looked up at Bannister. "The body has a penis," declared the pathologist. To emphasise his point, he drew back the modesty sheet, briefly exposing the lower part of the victim. He replaced it and continued. "The victim died instantly, with a serrated knife through the heart, which was then twisted inside the body. The injuries to the head and face occurred after death with a hammer…"

"The subject we had under surveillance was female," interjected Bannister gain. Turning to his partner. "Bob, did you see if the runner was male or female?"

"I don't know. As I said, the runner wore a black hoodie tied at the neck. I didn't see the face."

"Did the guy run like a girl?"

"I have no idea. It was frigging dark," Pullman shot back, getting annoyed.

"Gentlemen," boomed the voice from the dissecting table. "I do not have time to listen to your bickering. Do you want to know about this body or NOT?"

"I apologise, Mr Saur," said Bannister. "We are surprised the victim on your table is not the person we were observing. Please carry on."

"Thank you," Sour said sarcastically, and continued with his findings. "… or some kind of blunt metal instrument. He was a fit young man of possibly eastern European descent. His stomach contents are clean, and although he does not appear to have eaten recently, there is nothing sinister in his body. There is no trace of alcohol, and it is unlikely that he has taken drugs, but we will have to wait for toxicology reports to be certain."

"You said he was fit. Could he have been a sportsman?" asked Pullman.

"There is a possibility that he *was* some kind of sportsman. I am thinking, something like a boxer or martial arts performer. His whole body was muscular, which only come with extensive training. He had strong stomach muscles, meaning they were strengthened to take blows to the abdomen," ventured Mr Saur. "There are no traces of drugs, and he was a nonsmoker. I will tell you more when I have finished the autopsy, along with the toxicology report. Call me back in twenty-four hours."

"One more question, if I may, sir," asked Bannister. "There was not as much blood as I would have expected after the face and head had been so badly battered. Could you explain why not, please?"

"The victim was killed instantly, through the heart. With no pumping mechanism to push the blood around the body, the only blood you will find is that which dripped on to the floor from the skull and a small amount from the entry wound below the heart."

"Thank you, Mr Saur. We look forward to reading your report," replied Bannister. "I assume that samples of the dead man's blood have already been sent to the lab to try to trace identification.?"

"They have, detective."

Chapter Four

The two men returned to the station. Once back at their desks, they assembled in Monkhouse's office. The trio analysed the events of the last couple of days as Bannister and pullman reported their findings to the boss. Monkhouse listened in dismay as his detectives gave him the low down on the previous day's events. Including their time with Peter Saur.

"At least she was not on the morgue table."

Billy Monkhouse nodded. But he looked and sounded upset about someone he put on a search watch.

"So, we have lost Isobel Cooper," he said, running his finger through his silver hair. "Do you know the importance of finding her?" he asked the two men in front of him.

Bannister stared at his boss, while on the other chair, Pullman fingered with a bunch of keys. "No, boss. You have not told us the reason why you wanted us to put a surveillance on the girl, he said as he waited for an answer.

Monkhouse hesitated before answering, and it was not the answer Bannister was looking for. "For now, I can't tell you. orders from above," he lied. Monkhouse did not convince Bannister with his answer. He had a gut feeling his boss was lying.

The two men had known each other from cadet school. Bannister always wanted to be a detective, getting involved in the action. Monkhouse, however, craved the ambition to get to the top on the administrative side of policing and become a Chief Inspector, which he did after a spell on the beat.

Bannister was becoming frustrated with the lack of information. "Boss, if you want us to get on top of this quickly, we need more to go on and some extra back up. Because I smell rats which will come out of some big hole and bite us in the arse. Billy, we need more information as to what we are looking for," said Bannister forcefully, staring out Monkhouse.

Monkhouse returned the stare of his old friend. He appeared to be checking his temper and ready to explode, his face turned red. Taking a long sigh, he said, "The bloody powers that be won't release the cash which the home office promised to the department. I can't spare the resources," he lied once more. "I have to pick and choose where the money goes. Some cases get shoved to the bottom of the pile, sometimes never to see the light of day, and hope they disappear, and this is one of them. He cast his eyes to the ceiling in despair. "Sorry, guys. You will have to work with what you've got." He paused. "Find Isobel Cooper, and… she is important to…" His voice trailed away. "Just find her, please."

"But you can't tell us why?"

"No."

Without another word, the two detectives

nodded to their boss and left the office.

Billy Monkhouse watched his men leave. He hated not telling them the full story; it was not the time. He hated lying, especially to Malcolm Bannister. But for now, that's how it had to be. He did not get to this position by making easy decisions. At fifty-seven years old, he was three years away from retirement on a full pension. Monkhouse joined the force almost from when he left school. It was all he ever wanted to do. He met Bannister ten years later at a training course. They instantly became best friends.

From his beginnings as a police cadet, then after a stint on the beat, he worked his way steadily up the ladder to his current position. Unlike his friend, he did not relish the detective work, opting instead for a management career within the force. It was difficult at times, more so since he lost his wife, Angela, to cancer eight years ago. Malcolm pulled him through those dark times and was one of the pallbearers at Angela's funeral. But now, he had had enough. He wanted to sit out his remaining three years…quietly.

Chapter Five

Bannister lay awake on top of the covers of his bed, deep in thought. It was three in the morning, and although his body ached with exhaustion with the long and seemingly endless shifts, sleep would not come. With Monkhouse's words fresh in his mind about Isobel Cooper, and the way he said it, it didn't sound right. Bannister had a burning feeling, deep down, that the boss was holding something back and keeping it close to his chest. With precious little to go on, his mind was driving him crazy.

Who the hell was Isobel Cooper? His brain shouted at him. Why was the boss so vague?

He rose, made himself another mug of tea, and switched on the TV. After a few minutes of channel fiddling, he turned it off. Walking to the front window with his mug in hand, he stared at the black night sky, looking for inspiration. Clouds were forming, threating rain later.

Taking his tea back to bed, he set it by the bedside table. He lay back on the bed and pulled the covers over himself. Within minutes, he was fast asleep without finishing the tea.

He awoke with a start at the hammering on the front door. Fumbling with the alarm clock, he checked the time. "Fuck!" it was eight thirty. Either the alarm didn't go off or he slept so soundly that he didn't hear it. The hammering on the door continued. "Okay…okay, I'm coming." He shouted.

He checked through the peephole on the door before opening it. Bob Pullman stood on the landing with a frown on his face. "Are you okay?" he called.

"Yeah, yeah. Come in. put the kettle on while I get dressed."

"It's not like you to lie in, and we're meeting

Frankenstein at ten this morning."

"Oh shit! I couldn't sleep. Got up at three, made tea, then went back to bed at four." Bannister yawned. "This case is playing on my mind. I just can't shake it off. It stinks." He took the coffee from Pullman and winced at the first sip. "Jesus! Thank God you ain't married."

"I am married," he replied with a curious frown.

"What's on your mind, Malcolm?" asked Bob, grinning.

"This Cooper lass. We have to find her. Call in every snout, you know, especially in the drug and prostitute scene. She might be involved with them." Bannister was in a determined mood. "I have a feeling the is more to this than we know."

"I am not sure Sour will come up with anything new. He was very thorough. The dead guy's body was as clean as a whistle." Pullman remarked.

As Pullman made for the door, Bannister pour the remains of the coffee down the sink, then both men set off to the mortuary, late.

Through the huge glass window, Bob's *Frankenstein* was bent over another body splayed open on the stainless-steel table. At the sight of the two men standing at the window, Saur covered the body immediately.

"Ah, gentlemen, I was expecting you." his voice gain sent shiverers down Pullman's spine. "Although I expect punctuality. I do not have time to waste," he admonished them, looking up at the large morgue clock fixed on the white-tiled wall. They were seven minutes late.

Picking up a prepared report, he began. "As we discussed a few days ago, it would appear that your body was indeed a sportsman., something of a boxer. His stomach muscles, and indeed all of his muscles, were finely tuned, a well-tuned athlete. As you saw, he has a number of tattoos. But one caught my eye, which was set aside from the others. Suar pointed a remote at a screen high on one of the walls. "This," he said, "was tattooed high on his left shoulder."

The pathologist glanced at the two men,

squinting their heads as they stared at the figure of a dragon on the screen. "I brought it to your attention, as I thought it may have some significance to your investigation," he advised.

"What the hell is that?" asked Pullman.

"I have no idea," replied Saur, "That, gentlemen, is your department. And please do not swear in my mortuary, Mr Pullman. Have some respect for the dead."

"I apologise, Mr Saur," said an embarrassed Pullman, cringing.

"Thank you, Mr Saur," acknowledged Bannister. "You have been most helpful, and our apologies for our lateness and my partner's rudeness."

Peter Sau bowed ever so slightly, causing Pullman to shiver once more.

'That man is coming to get me.' "Let's get the

hell out of here," he hissed to his partner.

"I want to go back to Isobel Cooper's flat and see if we can turn up any further evidence or something we missed," suggested Bannister.

Chapter Six

The door to Isobel Cooper's flat was locked with a new padlock. Bannister, as the leading officer on the case, held a spare key. A length of yellow police tape stretched across the door, reading. 'POLICE DO NOT ENTER.'

Selecting a key from a bunch in his pocket. He opened the door. The victim's blood had been sanitised, and the rest of the rooms left as they were.

"I'll check the cleaner rooms first," suggested Bannister, putting on a pair of rubber gloves. Pullman did the same.

Pullman searched the kitchen, while his partner trolled through the single bedroom.

Neither man found anything new. "There has to be a clue in here somewhere," moaned Pullman.

"Okay. Let's search the murder room together. I don't want to miss an inch."

For two hours, the two detectives fine combed the room and frustratingly found nothing.

"Malcolm, do you notice anything missing?" asked Bob.

"No. Tell me."

"If Isobel Cooper is involved in drugs, and we don't know if she is, we should see some somewhere. And with our experience, we should smell the stuff, but there is none. He stood and stretched his back. "I am sure this case has to do with something other than drugs," he added.

"If there are any, they're probably stashed somewhere else. Keep looking." Bannister frowned, knowing his partner was right. "I'll call in the drugs squad with a dog for a final check."

"For a drug dealer, if she is one, she keeps the flat in immaculate condition, with almost nothing out of place. Even the drawers and cupboards are neat, the sign of a disciplined person. *This girl is house-proud.* Pullman observed. "If it ain't drugs, what the hell are we searching for?" he asked, exasperated.

"Maybe we'll get a clue from this," said Bannister, smiling, as he pulled out a red eight-inch iPad, which he found hidden, taped to the underside of one of the drawers. He pressed a button on the side of the iPad, which sprang to life. As expected, a password was required. He switched off the item and slipped it into an evidence bag. "I'll send it to forensics to trace it for prints."

Handing the iPad to a constable on watch, he said. "Get this to the station and the geeks. I don't want to waste passwords trying to get in. It maybe password limited to the maximum of times we can try."

"I can't see anything else showing up in here," commented Pullman. "The place is too clean."

Bannister nodded his agreement. "Let's go."

Back at the station, the forensics team had produced an identikit picture of the dead man's face, even through the gore! The guy looked more Asian than Eastern European. Bannister had a bunch of copies printed and passed out to the force in the hope that someone would recognise him. In the meantime, he and his partner scoured boxing gyms and martial arts centres in the area, but drew a blank.

There was a message from 'Frankenstein' waiting for them on their return, with more information on the body…

'The victim's toxicology has reported no traces of drugs of any kind in his body, not even muscle stimulants. This man had been a dedicated sportsman who took good care of himself. I would say possessively so. Blood samples show he was Middle Eastern, possibly Pakistani, Iraqi or Iranian. We also screened the blood and fingerprints through all known data banks and have drawn a blank. It appears this man does not exist.'

Bob Pullman shuddered as he read the report

from Saur. *I hate that creep.*

Chapter Seven

There was a knock on Bannister's office door. Allan Beasley, head of the station's IT department, opened Cooper's iPad with starting results. "We found nothing of interest on the phone you found under the dead guy. But I discovered this and remembered seeing this emblem in the pathologist's report." He set the iPad on the desk in front of the two men.

"It is the same tattoo that is on the victim's shoulder. We need to show these to the boss. This is becoming more sinister and intriguing, and I've got an uneasy feeling," commented Pullman.

Bannister nodded subconsciously as he listened to his partner. He continued to stare at the symbol, trying to figure out what he was looking at.

'*Something is in there!*' In the symbol. Something which was not hitting him. He turned to the IT chief. "Allan, can you send one of your geeks up here, please? I need a picture blown up.".

"Sure can." He picked up a phone on Bannister's desk. "Paul, can you come to the detectives' room, please?"

Minutes later, Malcolm was looking up at Paul Wilson and smiled. A twenty-three-year-old guy appeared in front of him. He looked as though he was a teenager still at school. He was very skinny, with a huge pair of round wire specs perched at the end of his nose as if they were ready to fall off. He was one hundred per cent geeky, and he was a cop.

"Hi, I am DC Bannister."

"Pleased to meet you. I am IT Wilson," he

attempted at a joke.

Bannister glowered at him, then turned the iPad to him with the picture of the dragon symbol on the screen. "Can you enlarge this symbol, please?"

Paul Wilson stood, staring down at the figure on the pad, seemingly unsure what to do our what to say.

The two detectives waited. "Paul, are you okay?" asked Pullman.

"Y…yeah," he replied, shaking his head as he came out of his reverie.

"Can you blow up the picture for us, please?" Pullman repeated.

"Yes, I can." Wilson fiddled with some of the iPad keys and the picture came to life in his hands.

"I can't see any difference," said Bob as the symbol grew larger.

Malcolm continued to fix his stare at the figure. "Can you focus more? On the centre"

"What is that?" asked Bannister, pointing to what looked like a smudge in the centre wing of the dragon in black script. "I need more."

"I could try to brighten it," suggested Paul.

After a few more minutes working on the keys, he came up with this...

"Wow! Now we are getting somewhere. Well done young man," said Bannister, patting him on the back.

"It looks like some kind of Arabic writing," said Paul, bending closer. "But I don't understand what it means."

"Do we know of anyone who works in the station that can speak Arabic?" asked Pullman.

"One of the girls I work with, Meera

Dhariwal. She may be able to speak Arabic," said Paul.

Immediately, Bannister called the IT department. "Alan, can you send down your girl, the one who can speak Arabic, please? I need her to translate a word for me."

"Did someone ask for me?" a voice quietly asked, almost in a whisper behind Bannister.

Bannister looked up from his desk at an olive-skinned girl in a policewoman's uniform and wearing a short dark blue jihad covering her head, standing in front of him.

"Hello, I am Meera Dhariwal," she introduced herself.

"Yes. I did. Thank you for coming down," pointing to the dragon tattoo on the iPad, he asked, "Do you recognise this symbol?"

After peering at the screen for a few moments, Meera drew back from the desk, seemingly afraid of what she was looking at.

"Well?" persisted Bannister.

"No…no, not the symbol," she stammered.

Bannister sensed she was lying and afraid. Whether it was the dragon figure or the writing, he wasn't sure at the moment.

Meera did not reply but continued to fix her gaze on the iPad in front of her.

"Meera. Look at me," said Pullman, coming round beside her. He sat on the edge of the table, facing her. Looking into her wide-open eyes, he asked softly, "I want you to look at that tattoo and tell me if you have seen it before. Can you do that?"

By now, the girl was shivering.

"The writing, Meera, what does it mean? Can you translate it?" Pullman asked softly, sensing the discomfort in the girl.

Paul, who was standing close by, put his hand on her arm. "It's okay. Just tell them what they want to know, if you can."

"Meera…?" The girl was clearly frightened at the sight of the symbol, and yet she had not seen the word which Malcolm wanted her to translate. Hitting a key on the iPad, he brought up the word on to the screen which Paul had enlarged … اغ ڌ يال. "…will you look at the Arabic word for me, please?" Bannister was treading carefully with the young IT policewoman.

She sighed deeply and nodded. "Yes, I will look." and forced her eyes on to the screen. "It is too dark to read."

Just then, Superintendent Monkhouse entered the room. "I am only here as an observer," he whispered, "please carry on."

"Shit," Bannister muttered under his breath. "That's all I need!" There are too many people in here, and the sight of the chief will only scare the girl more. He thought.

As Bob Pullman brought the enlarged and brighter Arabic word on to the screen, he turned it to face Meera. The three men glanced at each other and over at the frightened girl.

"Sit down, Meera," said Bannister, pulling over a chair. "Bob, some water." With a shaking hand, Meera sipped at the glass of water handed to her.

"You know what this is, don't you?"

She nodded her head. "The writing, yes."

Again, Pullman spoke to her quietly, trying to draw an answer from her, "What does it mean? It is an Arabic word, isn't it?"

"It is Arabic for 'assassin'," she finally replied, bowing her head. "Can I go now, please?" asked Meera, standing and stepping away from the screen.

"Yes. you can go for now," said Bannister, "But we may want to ask you some more questions later."

The men watched her walk away with Paul Wilson. The earlier spring in her step had gone.

"Do you think she knows something?" asked Monkhouse, who was standing behind Bannister.

"Without a doubt. I want to question her more when I have got my head around this." Bannister's eyes followed the girl until she was out of sight, with his brain working overtime.

He looked at Monkhouse. "Boss, do you have anything for me?"

His boss shook his head and left the room.

Chapter Eight

Two days later, Malcolm Bannister phoned Alan Beasley. "Can you send Meera down to me, please? I need a few words with her."

"She has not come in since you spoke to her the other day. In fact, she did not come back to the office after talking to you guys."

"Is she supposed to be on duty?"

"Yes."

"What's her address?" Instantly Bannister got to his feet. "Come on, Bob, I think Meera might be in trouble." As he grabbed his jacket and ran to the door, he shouted to one of his colleagues at a desk nearby. "Get back up over to Meera's place. RIGHT NOW."

THE HASSASSINI

In the carpool yard, the two partners commandeered a marked police car each, and with blues and twos blaring, they sped to Meera Dhariwal's house.

They reached her place in minutes; the girl lived a walking distance of the police station. The uniforms were already there, waiting by their cars as Bannister and Pullman ran to the house. Both detectives unholstered their Glocks, ready to face any complications. Bannister hammered at the front door as Pullman peered through the windows.

Seeing a hand on the floor close to a bedroom door, Pullman yelled at his partner. "She's down Malcolm! On the floor. Get an ambulance here fast," yelled Pullman as he ran round to the front of the house.

"Shit! Surround the building, guys. I'm going in." A champion weightlifter in his younger days and at six foot four, Bannister was a mountain of a man who still kept himself in reasonable shape. Shouldering the door several times, he made short work of breaking the lock from its moorings and splintering the door frame.

Meera, still in her police uniform, lay in a drying pool of blood which had poured from her severed jugular. She had bled out in minutes. Her blood flowed across the parquet flooring, then spread along the skirting boards on the uneven floor.

Rigor mortis had completed, with the body beginning to swell. The girl's throat had been cut, almost severing her head from her body. *'This was a professional hit,'* thought Bannister. He grimaced at the sight. In all his years in the force, it was something he could never get used to. Especially when there is so much blood and gore.

Pullman rushed in quickly behind his partner. Taking one look at Meera's body, he turned away and thumped his head in frustration on the bedroom doorpost with tears welling in his eyes. "We should have watched her. The girl knew something about that symbol, and she was too scared to tell us what it means. Fuck," cried an exasperated Pullman.

Within minutes, an ambulance appeared

outside the house. The paramedics rushed in, not having been told that the victim was already dead. Bannister stopped them and asked if they would wait until forensic completed their work.

Almost directly behind the paramedic, Superintendent Monkhouse walked into the room in full uniform. With his cap placed under his arm, he stared down at the body of Meera Dhariwal for several minutes, but said nothing. Bannister and his partner were surprised to see the appearance of the boss.

"Sir," Bannister acknowledged.

"Carry on," he ordered grimly, then turned and began to walk out of the house.

The two partners looked at each other with the same question on their minds. *What the hell was that all about?*

Pullman reacted before he left. "Sir."

Monkhouse stopped and faced his detective. "Yes?"

"Does this have anything to do with the

Cooper case?"

"I have no further comment." With that, he left the building.

Once the forensic team had finished processing Meera Dhariwal's body and the immediate scene around it, three paramedics carefully lifted the dead girl's remains into a black body bag. One of the paramedics held Meera's loose, almost severed head as the three men gently placed her remains in the black bag and zipped it closed.

"Malcolm. What the hell is he hiding? Do we have any call to bring the boss in for questioning?"

"I don't think so at this stage. He must have a hell of a good reason to behave this way. Let's hang fire and plough through this the best we can."

Chapter Nine

Bannister, along with Pullman and Monkhouse, stood at the large mortuary window looking down at the lifeless body of Meera Dhariwal lying on Peter Saur's stainless steel table covered in a white sheet.

    Saur had already completed the autopsy and was about to deliver the body to her family quickly, in accordance with the religious practices of the family. Grimly, he faced the three men on the level above him. Pulling out the report from underneath the table, he began. "Gentlemen, as you saw, the obvious cause of death was exsanguination, due severing of the carotid artery. The cut was particularly vicious, cutting through the spinal cord, almost severing the head from the body. This appears to be a professional killing. The weapon was probably a military knife. An ordinary knife would not be capable of causing this kind of injury. Death will have been almost instantaneous." Saur hesitated to check his note before continuing. "There are also some fresh bruises on different parts of her skin, showing she was slapped and punched moments before her death. She died approximately sixty hours ago on the spot where you found her."

Bannister did a quick calculation in his head. *That was the day almost to the hour when we interviewed her.* Then he thought. *Who knew she was being interviewed outside of the police station?*

Peter Saur completed, "In according with the religious beliefs of the family, and because we know the precise cause of death, it was not necessary to perform a total autopsy."

Bannister turned his attention back to the pathologist's monologue.

Pointing to the screen directly above Meera's body. "I did find this tattoo on the upper part of her left shoulder, similar to the one on the dead guy you found a couple of days ago."

All eyes stared at the screen in shock at the sight of the second dragon symbol.

"Oh my God," Bill Monkhouse gasped. "She and this organisation may have infiltrated our computers." Snapping open his mobile, he called Allan Beasley. "Seal off Meera Dhariwal's computer and workstation…NOW," he commanded, his voice shaking with anger.

This was a side to Monkhouse that Bannister had never witnessed in the thirty years he had known his friend. His normally calm boss seemed frightened.

Turning to the two detectives, Monkhouse instructed, "Bannister, you and Pullman, get back and see what damage has been done and ask Beasley to contain it."

"I don't like the look of this," said Pullman. "this is turning out to be more than the simple surveillance operation we started a few days ago."

"Yeah," replied his partner, "and still Monkhouse is not telling us enough."

"We need to interview him officially."

"Not yet, but let's build a case, and then we will compare notes. But I still want to wait a few more days before doing anything or calling in the IOCP."

Chapter Ten

"Have you found any new leads, Allan?" asked Pullman, hovering over Meera Dhariwal's computer as it was being checked by Beasley, the station's IT manager. Bannister stood by his side.

"Nahh. This is as tight as hell," answered Beasley, shaking his head in frustration. "The girl knew what she was doing. Everything is as clean as a whistle…" he added, "It looks too clean. I can usually find mistakes in any of the computers in this office, if I look hard enough. But not here."

"And Meera? Is there anything to go on about the poor girl? Work history. Family, anything?"

"What we have found out so far is this…," replied Beasley, snapping open his notebook. "…

a sponsor assessed her and procured the position for the girl as a trainee operative in our IT department. I had no say in the interview. I was 'obliged' to take her on and give her, her own workstation almost immediately." Beasley looked for the men's reactions before continuing. "She studied computer science at Birmingham university, graduating with first degree honours and almost top of the class. She was one of the best operatives in the unit. I was considering her early for a promotion."

"Who was the sponsor?" asked Bannister.

"That's the strange thing; there is no mention of the sponsor's name. Inspector Monkhouse came to the office with her and gave me the information, and she started immediately."

"Home history?"

Beasley continued reading from his notes. "Meera was a British national from third generation Pakistani parents. Her great-grandfather came over to Britain in the exodus after the second world war. He worked as a London bus driver. About ten years ago the family moved to here, in Glasgow." Allan hesitated. "Now here is the rub. Both parents were murdered here, in the house seven years ago, when Meera was out with friends. She was nineteen then."

"That makes her twenty-six now," interjected Bannister.

Beasley nodded and went on, "Meera discovered the bodies of her parents when she returned home after an evening out with friends. By then, the killer or killers had disappeared. At the time, the police suspected that it could have been an 'honour' killing because the parents had opted out of an arranged marriage for Meera. It was thought that was why they move from London to Glasgow. It was assumed the killers would have left the country immediately after the murders. The case was shelved as unsolved."

"How did they die?" asked Bannister.

"The killers slashed her parent's throats viciously, almost the same way as Meera and the stranger in Isobel Cooper's flat died!"

"What?"

"And that's not all," added Beasley. "The postmortem pathologist suggested a military-style weapon killed them, i.e. an army knife."

"Shit! The bastards are back in the country."

"Maybe they never left," suggested Pullman. "A cell in waiting for orders."

"There is no way all these killings were a coincidence," Bannister said. *But why did they spare Meera?* He wondered. Turning to Allan Beasley, he asked, "Did she have any siblings?

"She had a brother, two years younger. He disappeared at the same time as his parent's murder. The feeling is that he was taken back to Pakistan as a revenge for the honour and sold or married into a family over there."

"And?"

"We are trying to trace him. Relations with the police in Pakistan are difficult, and so far, we have come up with nothing," said Beasley.

Bannister sighed. "Keep the guys trying and step up communications with the Pakistani police in light of this. He could be useful if he is still alive."

Chapter Eleven

Bannister and Pullman adjourned to the office to ponder over the case. As they scanned computers, their boss, Superintendent Monkhouse, slid into a chair next to them. Bannister eyed him with suspicion.

"Who have we got on the inside?" asked Monkhouse. "We need someone with Asian connections."

"There is a snout I use called Abdul Zahir," said Pullman.

"Can he be trusted?"

"Can anyone?"

Bannister grimaced. "Touche. Get him to the

station, now!"

"Nahh! He won't show his face in a cop shop," added Pullman. "I'll try to arrange a meeting in a safe house." An hour later pullman reported back to his partner. "He won't meet at the safe house either, but he has offered to meet at a place of his choosing."

"In that case, fine. But do we know if *we* will be safe?"

"I'll arrange discreet backup for you," Monkhouse offered, "and also, I want to be there."

The partners looked at each other. "Sure, boss."

When Monkhouse left the office, Bannister raised his concerns with his partner. "I have never known the boss to be so involved in a case the way he has with this one. I am becoming more suspicious by the day, and I do not like where this might lead.

The trio met with Abdul Zahir in a hotel

opposite the main city mosque. He was an untidy little guy about five foot four with a full beard. He wore clothes which looked as though they had not been cleaned since God knows when. And baggy trousers halfway up his ankles.

Billy Monkhouse arrived casually dressed in a herringbone jacket and black trousers. His white shirt was unbuttoned two buttons down at the neck.

Zahir was waiting for them in the reception area. He looked scared. Bannister approached the reception desk, flashed his ID, and asked for a room with a table and chair.

In the room, Bannister took Zahir's outstretched hand as Pullman introduced them. He did not shake the snout's hand, but released the guy's clammy fingers immediately. He took an instant dislike to Pullman's snout.

Introductions over, Zahir sat opposite the three cops, nervously tapping the table with his right hand and holding a set of worry beads on his left.

Pullman pulled out his iPhone and placed a

picture of the dragon symbol in front of Zahir.

Instantly, the slimy guy stared up at Pullman, his eyes widened… "Noooo!" He turned and headed for the door. Looking back at the three cops, he screeched, almost screaming. "I want nothing to do with that; you should not have shown that to me!" he screamed at them, his voice shaking in fear.

As he put his hand on the doorknob, Bannister grabbed him by the arm, while Pullman pulled up a chair and thudded it in the middle of the room.

Bannister shoved Zahir, who was no match for the bigger man, down into the chair. The skinny man's eyes were wide with terror.

The big detective picked up another chair, and with the back of the chair facing Zahir, he straddled it like a cowboy. He folded his arms on the backrest, leaned forward and glared into the face of the snout. For four tense minutes, Bannister remained fixed in one position…silent, staring into his eyes. Zahir lolled his head around the room, trying to avoid the big man's intense stare, squirming on the chair as the cop glared him out.

Finally… "Tell me what this is?" Bannister demanded as he reached behind him, took the iPhone from Pullman, and shoved it under the eyes of Zahir.

The scared man looked at the symbol and shook his head. "I don't know."

"You don't know or won't tell me?" Bannister's foot shot out and kicked a leg of the chair which Zahir was sitting on. The frightened man had been leaning forward, holding his head in both hands. He sat up sharply as the cop's foot thudded into the chair leg.

"They will kill me if I say anything. Let me out of here. I have done nothing," he pleaded.

"Then you DO KNOW something!" Bannister pressed on him, moving closer, their faces almost touching.

"Pleeease."

Bannister shook his head. "Nope. Just tell me what this is, and I'll open the door for you myself and you can go."

Zahir continued to shake his head, with tears streaming down his face, said nothing.

Turning to his partner, Bannister said, "Bob, read the guy his rights with the list of charges we can pin on this him to keep him in a cell, 'til he talks?'"

"Oh sure. The problem is, if we put him with the other cons, they will suss he is a grass…and we have seen what happens to snouts who grass."

"I…I…I. Oh, Allah, help me," Zahir cried, raising his eyes to the ceiling.

"Allah will help you when you help us," said Pullman.

Zahir was sweating profusely. "The dragon is the symbol of a group called The Hassassini," he said, shivering.

"Now we are getting somewhere." Bannister smiled, getting up from his chair and pushing it aside. Zahir made a move to rise, but Bannister pushed him back down. "We are not finished with you yet."

"Who are The Hassassini?" Pullman asked with a frown. "And what does it mean?"

"Hassassini is an ancient Arab word for an assassin," blubbered Zahir.

Looking at Monkhouse, Bannister remarked, "This is a new one boss. We have nothing of this organisation on our databases."

"They are an elite creed within the brotherhood. They kill to order, but target those whom they consider traitors to our cause." By now, Zahir was a broken man.

"Who is their next target? Bannister barked.

"I don't know," he replied with a deep sigh. "The Hassassini does not get told until the last moment who his target is." Zahir wrung his hands. "No…no, enough! I will say no more."

"How many are there?"

"They are many and everywhere, always at the end of a phone, waiting for the next assignment. Please let me leave," he begged.

Pullman and Banister left the room. "I don't think we will get anywhere further with this guy. Let him go and have him followed," suggested Pullman.

Bannister nodded. "Okay, let's try that. keep him here a little longer while we get a surveillance team set up."

Ten minutes later, after some more fruitless questioning, Bannister hauled Zahir to his feet. "Get out. But stay close. We will want to talk to you again."

"Thank you…thank you, the snout said as he left the room in a hurry.

As the three men were discussing the case. There was a loud sound of a car crash outside the hotel, along with people screaming.

The trio rushed to the window. Two cars had crashed, but a crowd was gathered around a body lying on the pavement.

"Pullman, go and check what is happening," asked the superintendent.

From the street below, Pullman rang Monkhouse. "It's Zahir, sir, he's dead."

Pullman checked with witnesses as to what happened, then related his findings to the two men. "Two guys on a motor bike drove up close to him. The passenger struck Zahir on the back of the neck with a machete. His head is hanging from his body by the skin."

Chapter Twelve

Bannister and Pullman sat in a huddle, pondering the case over pints in the local watering hole. It was Pullman who spoke first.

"We've three dead guys and a missing female. Add to that the murders of Meera's parents, and an unknown symbol of an assassin cell, called 'The Hassassini,' who may be here on a killing mission. But we don't know who the intended victim is." Pullman let his thoughts sink in as he swallowed another slug of his pint. "This mystery dead guy in Isobel's flat, Malc, I wonder if he had been brought here to assassinate someone, was discovered and killed? And to top it all. What the fuck is Monkhouse's involvement in all of this? Now, that is frustrating me. I am sure he knows more than he is telling."

The two sat in silence, deep in their own thoughts.

"Malc, we have barely mentioned the missing Isobel Cooper. Where does she fit into all of this? Is she a Hassassini?"

Bannister sat up, swirled his beer around the half empty glass and screwed his face. "Bob, that is a possibility. If they sent our mystery guy to kill someone, but who? And if they are so determined to carry it out, then you can bet there will be other assassins waiting to take his place, according to Zahir. But Cooper? I dono. I just wish the boss would tell us more."

Bob nodded in agreement. "I called Alan Beasley. He double checked, there was nothing called 'The Hassassini' in any database. They seem to be a secretive creed."

"Or a new one."

Pullman added, "There is something about the IT guy I don't trust. What's his name again?"

"Paul Wilson," Bannister replied, "I developed a suspicious feeling about him too, right from the beginning, when we showed him the dragon symbol. He knows more than he is letting on. I want him in the office first thing in the morning."

"I agree," said Pullman. "He might be one of our missing links. Wilson has known Meera Dhariwal for the best part of three years. They worked together in the same office next to each other. You can't be that close to someone for a length of time without getting to know some of each other's personal habits."

"Or share a drink or two over technical issues that I know fuck all about! Jesus. I am getting old, and I am heading for bed. G'night buddy."

"Malc, calling Wilson, could put him at risk."

"Yeah," replied Bannister, "but only if it implicates him. And if he is, I will fry his ass in the morning."

Chapter Thirteen

At eight am the following morning, Monkhouse joined a refreshed Bannister and Pullman ready for action in a secure interview room. Pullman called up the geek from the IT office.

Before Wilson arrived, Bannister addressed his two colleagues. "Guys, this case has become more serious and confusing, and we need to get a handle on it before anyone else gets killed. Right now, there is little to go on, and I want to lean on Wilson.

"As far as I can see, he is our only *living* link connecting us to this case. So far, there have been at least three killings. Each has two common denominators, the dragon symbol, and the word Hassassini." Bannister paused for effect. "Wilson is our only hope at the moment of breaking through before anyone gets to him."

Looking at the boss, Pullman said, "We believe they are targeting someone for assassination. Who it is, we don't yet know. We assume that this dead stranger in Isobel Cooper's flat…" Bannister drew a look at his boss to see if there was any reaction before continuing. "… is a member of the 'Hassassini Creed,' and was sent over to kill a prominent Muslim, but he was found out, and paid the price. Again, we have no idea who the intended victim will be, but it may be one of their own."

Pointing to a computer screen he went on, "this group, with the dragon symbol tattooed on their shoulders, is aggressive, ruthless, and suicidal. We have seen what they are capable off, therefore, we need to find out who the target is and who the assassin will be."

The room door opened, and Paul Wilson jauntily walked in, unaware he would be interrogated. His cockiness raised Bannister's suspicions further, that he might have something to tell them. The detective told him to sit on a metal chair in front of the table.

Turning to the young IT operative. Bob Pullman started the interview. "Has anyone been near Meera Dhariwal's computer and workstation since your boss sealed it off?" Pullman asked.

"Not while I have been there," he smiled. There was something about his smile that sent shivers through Bannister.

"What do you know about Meera's private life?"

"N… nothing. I only see her when we come to work."

Bannister sensed the lie in Wilson's voice. Call it a gut feeling, police intuition, or whatever. He was not convinced by Paul Wilson's reply.

"Oh, come on Paul. You have worked with her for how long? Three years? And she told you nothing about her personal life?" insisted Pullman.

"I did not work *with* her, sir. I worked beside her. Meera and I worked on separate assignments," Paul smiled as he answered, but the cockiness was waning.

Bannister looked across at his boss, who was sitting aside from his two detectives. Monkhouse gave a slight knowing nod to Bannister to step up the ante, which Wilson hadn't noticed.

It's time to wipe that smile off your face, sonny. Bannister thought. Rising from his chair, Bannister drew up to his six-foot-four frame and towered over Wilson. "Look, son, don't make this difficult. I can tell that you are lying. After working with the *dead* girl for over two years, you must know something about her. So, I will repeat detective Pullman's question. What do you know about Meera Dhariwal? Any snippets of information will be of help," he said with a grin.

"Dead? I didn't know she was dead!" said the shocked IT geek, sitting up straight. "I only worked beside her," he repeated, this time without the smile on his face, as his fear became more prevalent.

Bannister leaned his bulk down closer to Wilson, causing him to lean back on his chair and almost tip over. "Oh yes, they got your friend, cut her throat they did," Bannister went on, drawing his thumb across the geek's throat, "and you know who it was."

Wilson tried to rise. "I want out of here. This has nothing to do with me." But the bigger man gripped his left shoulder and pushed him back. "Hey, you can't do that," Wilson protested. "I know the rules of questioning. I read up on them for my police exams."

"Hmmm, have you now?" mocked Pullman. "that will be the written rules then?" he added.

Wilson nodded his head. He was shaking as he looked at his hands. Scared.

"What about the unwritten rules? Did you read them?"

"Wha…what unwritten rules? You can't read rules that haven't been written! And you can't make them up as you go along."

Monkhouse shrugged his shoulders as Wilson looked over at him for support. Instead, Monkhouse told him, "I am suspending you from duties at your computer. Later, someone from another force will dissect your work and that of your dead colleague, who, by the way, was cut from ear to ear, if you remember Sergeant Pullman telling you. I will ask you one more time. Is there anything you want to say to these two gentlemen before I leave the room and let them get on with the 'unwritten rules?' Did you share any information with Meera Dhariwal?"

"No…no."

"Liar," called Pullman, as the questioning became more aggressive.

"What did you share?" Bannister slapped a blown-up picture of the dragon in front of Wilson, which made the young man jump, "What is that?" Bannister asked him… loudly.

"I don't know. It is just a tattoo Meera had on her shoulder."

Malcolm Bannister smiled inwardly. *Got him.* "So, you did share information?" The big man shouted into his ear. Bannister had caught him out. It was the geek's first mistake.

"No…no…no. That is all Meera showed to me," he said, shaking his head.

"Where did you see it?" They were nose to nose as Bannister pressed home his question.

Wilson lowered his head, sobbing softly, "On her shoulder, her left shoulder."

"At her home?"

"No, in a hotel. We went for a meal and…" he shrugged.

"Did you have sex with her?"

"Yes."

Bannister glanced back at the two men. *Success.*

"I knew all along you were lying. First, you told us Meera showed you nothing and now you admit to this. What else did you share?" Bannister demanded to know. "What is this tattoo you saw on her shoulder? Did she tell you what it meant?"

"It…it's. Nooo! I…I don't know." Tears began to trickle down Paul Wilson's face.

Bannister could see he was now terrified and near to breaking point.

Superintendent Monkhouse picked up the phone and called Allan Beasley. "Secure Wilson's computer and work station...*now*. Touch nothing nor let anyone near his or Meera Dhariwal's desks until we get there."

Turning to Pullman, he said. "Arrest him."

Pullman pulled his cuffs from his belt, "Stand up," he ordered Wilson, "Paul Wilson, I am arresting you on suspicion of withholding information of a crime or crimes you know will be committed..."

Paul Wilson looked more relieved than surprised as he stood meekly to be cuffed and taken to a cell.

Chapter Fourteen

The Emirates A380 jet landed at Heathrow Airport, dead on time, with Hosani Islamabad on board. After a seven-hour flight from Riyadh airport in Dhubi, he disembarked before his connecting flight to Glasgow.

Hosani Islamabad stepped from the aircraft and into the corridor towards the check-in desk. The trip had been pleasant, but uneventful on board the Emirates Airline. As always, he travelled first class, a luxury he could well afford. His services were unique and efficient, and his fees reflected his expertise.

He travelled extensively when called upon by his masters', to go anywhere on the globe where his special talents were required. As always, he dressed and travelled like a well-bred businessman. He rarely travelled using the same alias twice. On each trip, his sponsor would provide him with new identities and new false passports. Money was never an object, and none of the aliases would overlap. Each trip would last only a few days or less, making it impossible for passport control in any country to trace him.

He smiled to the attractive hostess as he left the A380 aircraft and made his way to passport control, passing through the 'nothing to declare' section with no suspicious looks from the customs personnel. Islamabad was resplendent in his Armani dark blue business suit, striped shirt complete with gold cufflinks, wearing a silk tie, and carrying a black Buroni attaché case. He prided himself on his dress sense. He stood five foot eleven and was at his peak of fitness. An expert combatant, with a black belt in several martial arts disciplines, he could take good care of himself in any unforeseen eventualities.

On arrival at Glasgow airport in Paisley, Hosani deposited a small travelling case in the boot of the prearranged limousine, which awaited him at the terminal entrance, where a uniformed driver held the door open. Armed with a sufficient change of clothing for several days, the Hassassini was ready. He slipped his hand into his inside jacket pocket, checking that the details supplied by Meera Dhariwal before her death were still there. Unfortunately, the authorities in Scotland were getting too close to her. The poor girl had to be disposed of.

He would determine his weapon of choice when he reached his destination, but the silence of the knife was always his preferred weapon.

A brother would finance the trip and provide details of the intended victim. The assassin would not know his proposed target until the last minute. Then, the Hassassini would receive a package with photos of the victim, and a credit card with more than enough funds to carry out his mission. His fee would already have been transferred into his personal untraceable numbered account.

But, most important …He is a killer. He is a Hassassini, and one of the best.

Chapter Fifteen

Twelve hours after the first interview with Paul Wilson, Bannister had him brought to a secure room set aside from the normal interview rooms.

The dark green room was bare apart from a table and three chairs. They'd bolted the steel table and the metal chair to the floor. A metal bar was welded on top of the table, which would restrain a violent prisoner. With Wilson, that would not be necessary. Bannister's strength would be sufficient if needed.

Superintendent Monkhouse wanted to be involved in everything that took place in this case. An extra chair was placed in the left-hand corner of the room so he could watch the two men conduct the interrogation.

Paul Wilson was brought into the room, flanked by two policemen, and unceremoniously dumped on the steel chair. The two partners sat on the opposite side of the table. Pullman sat on the right of Bannister, while their boss sat on the chair in the left-hand corner of the room.

"Put both hands on the table," Bannister ordered.

Wilson looked at Bannister and did as he was told. Nervously, he gently placed each hand on either side of the metal bar, expecting to be handcuffed to it.

Pullman, who had said nothing thus far, pulled out his handcuffs, twirled them in his fingers for a few moments, and threw them onto the steel table. They landed with a loud clatter, causing Wilson to jump in his seat.

For a full five minutes, there was a rehearsed silence between the three policemen. They looked directly at the frightened Wilson as they worked on the geek's nerves. Bannister glanced at his watch and stood up. Walking over to the other corner of the room, he picked up an old police truncheon leaning against the wall.

"Y…you cannot use that," stammered Wilson, "this is not the CIA!"

Bannister ignored the frightened man's remark and walked behind him, slapping the truncheon into his left hand, at the same time looking towards Pullman and his boss.

Brushing the truncheon across the back of Wilson's neck, he nodded to the two men in readiness. Suddenly he slammed the truncheon hard down on the steel table, dangerously close to Wilson's fingers.

"Fuck!" Wilson screamed.

Monkhouse walked over to the table. Leaning forward with his elbows on the table, he put his face close to the prisoner. By now, Wilson was sure that he would be beaten by man-mountain Bannister.

"Look, son," began Monkhouse quietly, "Meera Dhariwal is dead, a stranger is dead, and a snitch is dead." He paused to let his words take effect. "Everything points to this dragon tattoo which you claim to know 'nothing' about."

Wilson eyed Bannister, who was circling the cell, still slapping the truncheon into his hand. "When and if we let you out of here...*you* will be dead! Not by us, but by whoever you are protecting. Whatever they have paid or offered you, you will not live to spend it. Now be a good lad and tell us everything you know, and we can protect you."

Monkhouse stood up, but Wilson was not for talking. The superintendent continued, "You do not understand what you are getting yourself into. You're a clever lad with a bright future ahead of you in the force. You're a bright fella. So just tell us what you and Meera told each other. Did she ask your advice on anything?"

Wilson bowed his head and shook it.

"Okay guys, he is all yours. Unwritten rules may apply," lied Monkhouse.

"Unbutton your shirt and show us your shoulders," ordered Pullman.

"Why?"

Bannister tapped the table menacingly with the tip of the truncheon. Paul Wilson glanced at it nervously. "Do it! Or I will rip the fucking shirt off your skinny back," the big man threatened behind him.

"I don't have any symbols on my should...." Realising his blunder, Wilson screamed hysterically, "I am saying no more until I've seen a solicitor!"

"Unwritten rules, sonny," Bannister reminded him and pulled the shirt from his shoulders, snapping off several buttons as he did so. "Clean, damn. There's no tattoo." He cursed as he looked down at the geek's pale, thin body.

Billy Monkhouse shoved a blank sheet of paper and a pen in front of him. "Write down everything you know about Meera Dhariwal, and what you both shared, and all you know about this dragon symbol. This is your last chance."

Wilson stared at the blank sheet of paper for a few long moments as the trio waited. He shook his head. "I want a solicitor."

"Son, in a case like this, your access to a solicitor is denied," advised Monkhouse. "In the interest of national security," he lied.

Bannister and Pullman looked at each other. They knew that the boss was lying, and both wondered why.

"Clap him into one of the special cells," said Monkhouse, loud enough for Wilson to hear, although most of the cells were the same.

Pullman once again cuffed Paul Wilson and led him meekly out of the room.

As Pullman led the guy away, Bannister phoned the duty sergeant. "Andrew, strip one of your cells bare. Take out everything: mattress, pillows, everything.

"Okay."

"When you book in the guy Pullman is bringing down, he has been told he is going into a 'special' cell. Keep him thinking that's what it is."

"There is an empty padded cell. Will that be okay?" suggested the duty sergeant.

"Even better," agreed Bannister. "By the way, he is a suspected rogue cop, one of ours. Rough him up a little."

Andrew raised his eyes. "Okay will do. White overall?"

"Yeah, good idea. I need to break him some more."

"We can hold him for forty-eight hours. Then we will have to charge or release him," Billy Monkhouse advised.

Malcolm Bannister nodded. "Boss, I am not sure of his chances of survival if he gets out of here."

"I know, but legally, there is nothing we can do," added the superintendent. "But I've a feeling he has unwittingly got himself caught up in the charms of Meera Dhariwal, and he is treading on dangerous ground."

Chapter Sixteen

At five in the morning on the following day, Bannister and Pullman opened the cell door. The cops had stripped Wilson of all of his clothing and garbed him in a white prison boiler suit.

A frightened and dishevelled Wilson cowered in the right-hand corner of his cell. He was shivering in a foetal position, with his arms curved around his doubled–up legs. Saliva dribbled from the corners of his mouth.

As Wilson looked up at the white-shirted Bannister, who had his sleeves rolled up ready for action, dried streaks of tears were visible down both sides of the lad's cheeks.

Pullman wondered if they had made a mistake

and were being too severe with the young geek.

Bannister stuck his head out of the cell door and yelled. "Sergeant!" Loud enough for the prisoner to hear.

"Sir?"

"Bring Wilson's clothing in here."

A constable brought the clothing to the cell and laid it on the bare metal bed.

"I'll leave you to get changed, Wilson. We will be back in five minutes after I had a word with the duty sergeant, so move your arse."

Pullman was waiting and chatting to the sergeant at the duty desk. "Do you think we are too tough on the youngster?" he asked his partner.

"No Bob. Three people are dead, and one girl is missing. I don't care how innocent or geeky he looks. He is hiding something, and I will fucking get it out of him. End of story."

Pullman sighed, still unsure.

Malcolm Bannister tried to put his partner's

mind at ease. "Everyone makes mistakes, Bob," he admitted to his colleague, "you and I do, too. But in this crazy world in which we live, it is better to be sorry than dead. And if that guy…" He pointed to Wilson's cell with his thumb. "…if that guy has passed on information to Meera Dhariwal, he is a fucking terrorist, just like the others."

Seven minutes later, the two men returned to the cell to collect Paul Wilson. The geek had not moved from where they last left him. He remained in the same foetal position, shivering and dribbling.

It was clear that something was wrong. "Get a medic in here, fast," shouted the duty sergeant down the hallway.

Meanwhile, Pullman slowly approached the still crouched Wilson. Putting his arms around his shoulders to calm him, he whispered quietly. "Easy lad. The doctor is coming to see you." He looked into Wilson's eyes, which were wide open and unblinking as he stared with hatred at Malcolm Bannister standing behind Pullman.

"Malcolm, I think you should make yourself

scarce for the time being. At least until he is seen by the doc," Pullman suggested.

Undeterred, Bannister glowered back into the eyes of the crouched geek. *He fucking knows more than he is telling.* He nodded without a word to his partner and left.

Billy Monkhouse called Bannister to his office. "Fill me in. This is getting out of hand. We have three killings, a missing woman, and now a traumatised IT operative, and somehow, they are all linked to this dragon tattoo or symbolic creed."

Bannister mused before answering. "For Paul Wilson to get into the state he has gotten himself into, and we both know I've interviewed thousands of people, it has to be more than his fear of me. I know it is an abject fear of something else."

Monkhouse leant forward with his elbows on the desk, hanging on to his colleague's every word.

Bannister went on, "Wilson knows more than he is telling. He is scared shitless, or he is one of them and he knows how ruthless this creed is, and what he knows has got him traumatised."

"Have you any leads on the missing girl, Isobel Cooper?" Monkhouse asked.

"No, she has gone to ground." Suddenly, Bannister sat bolt upright. "Sir, can I make a call?"

"Of course."

Punching in some numbers on his iPhone, Bannister put the phone to his ear. "Peter?"

"Yes," the Germanic voice replied.

"I need a favour, please."

"Which is?"

"Can you cross match two blood samples for me, please?" Bannister gave the pathologist the details of the samples he needed checked.

"Certainly. I will phone you in a few hours with the results, Mr Bannister."

"Thank you."

Billy Monkhouse looked at his detective, puzzled.

"I will give you the details when I get them, sir."

Chapter Seventeen

By the time the doctor got to Wilson's side, he had become almost comatose, and leaning to one side. Immediately, the doctor injected him with a relaxant. "Call an ambulance and get him to hospital fast!" the doc yelled. "He is totally in shock."

Medics strapped a sedated Paul Wilson to a stretcher and prepared to rush him to the hospital, watched closely by a still sceptic Bannister. As the detective saw him leave, he was sure he saw Wilson opened his right eye and quickly closed it again.

I fucking knew it! Fumed Bannister.

Immediately, he went int action and upped

the ante. "I want a full search team at Wilson's flat," declared Bannister to the desk sergeant.

Allan Beasley was astounded as he entered the flat. Paul Wilson's flat was typically geeky. Four computers surrounded the walls, and IT material of every description littered all around the flat. Hundreds of gaming paraphernalia were strewn throughout both rooms of the apartment. He was a serious games programmer in his spare time. And Beasley suspected he was a hacker, too.

Along with Bannister and Pullman, several police and IT experts gathered items of interest and then bundled everything they thought would be useful and into a waiting police van.

Pullman sniffed the air inside the flat. "That's a strange smell," he remarked to no one in particular. "It's not cannabis. I would recognise the smell of the weed anywhere."

"You're right Bob," Bannister confirmed.

"It's the smell similar to the kind you would find in a mosque, sir," remarked a young dark-skinned constable, "a kind of Asian odour, of spices."

"I knew that bastard Wilson was lying. Meera Dhariwal was in here," Bannister swore. "Shit! That makes him an accessory to murder, among other charges, if he didn't do it himself."

"Detective Pullman, you should see this." The same young cop pointed to one of the four computers he had switched on. The screen showed a picture of the dragon symbol.

"Thank you, constable," said Pullman. "We know about the dragon."

"Yes, sir. But look at the name below."

Bob Pullman moved closer to the computer screen. "Who is he?"

"This is a very famous man in our community. He lectures at my mosque. He also travels the country preaching peace to our young people, and trying to prevent them from being drawn into radicalisation," the young policeman explained. "But he also has enemies among the Jihadists because of what he is trying to do."

"Tomorrow, after *Youm Jumu'ah* or Friday prayers, he will give a speech to the young of the community. Many of our elders will be there too," explained the young cop.

Bannister's phone rang while he was in another room. He tapped it to life and put it to his ear. "Malcolm, we know who the target is and when," his partner revealed, his voice tingling with excitement. "It's tomorrow, Friday," Pullman said.

"Shit! Get to the hospital and Wilson fast," said Bannister. Then, turning to the others in the flat, he added, "Sweep this place, totally, take it apart. This is now a terrorist search."

Chapter Eighteen

Bannister glanced at the brightly lit screen on his iPhone. "Peter?"

"I have interesting information you requested, Mr Bannister. I am sorry that I did not think of it at the time," Peter Saur apologised.

Bannister bit his tongue, silently urging the pathologist to get on with it.

"We did the blood comparison as requested."

Come on…come on, spit it out.

"The dead victim at Isobel Cooper's flat, and your murdered police operative, Meera Dhariwal, were brother and sister!"

The missing sibling, thought Bannister. "Thank you, Peter. That will be most helpful." Bannister smiled to himself. *At last, we are getting somewhere.* He sighed, his heart pounding. *Shit, I am getting too old for this.*

"Bob," he called his partner. "Meera and the dead guy at the flat were brother and sister. They were both involved in the possible assassination of this guy on Friday at the mosque."

"It would appear that they were drawn into the Hassassini creed after their parents were murdered," surmised Pullman.

Chapter Nineteen

A sedated Paul Wilson lay in a hospital bed in one of the private side wards, with a cop on guard outside the door. Several doctors examined him, observed by a police medic. He was found to be physically fine, but there were concerns about his immediate mental state. They transferred him to a private psychiatric ward, where a consultant psychiatrist examined him.

Wilson was left to sleep with a drip attached to his left arm. With the doctors gone, a nurse fussed around him, making him comfortable, and checking his drip. In the meantime, the cop rushed off for a quick toilet break.

Walking to a worktop, the nurse busied herself by sorting out his medications for later. With her back to the door, and with the noise of the humming coming from an air conditioner, the nurse did not hear the approaching intruders. Two men, both dressed in stolen hospital scrubs, pushed a trolley into the ward.

While one of them positioned the trolley against the side of Wilson's bed, the other approached the unsuspecting nurse from behind. With an arm around her shoulder and a quick twist of her neck, the girl died instantly.

The two fake doctors bundled Paul Wilson on to the trolley along with the drip bottle. No one gave them a second glance as they wheeled him to the exit and into a waiting private ambulance. The extraction took only a couple of minutes.

As the ambulance drove off, Bannister and Pullman sped into the accident and emergency department, leaving the police car in the care of the young constable. Both men rushed to the psych ward.

"Shit!" Swore Bannister as they barged into the empty ward. "Why was there no guard on Wilson?" He noticed the drip holder without the drip bottle. "They are keeping him alive…God help him."

"Malcolm," Pullman pointed to the nurse, half hidden under a white sheet.

"Now four people are dead. We have to end this now!" said Bannister.

* * *

Paul Wilson opened his eyes. Looking up at his captors looming over him on the trolley, he grinned, "Am I glad to see you guys?"

He made to rise and get off the trolley, but one of the men roughly shoved him down again. The drip bottle was raised onto a makeshift hanger. "Hey, what's going on? I gave you what you wanted. I gave Meera the details of the preacher guy's timetable. All I want is the payment that you promised me, and then I will be gone."

As one of the men set up the drip, the other told him, "But now you know too much. The creed has no more use for you." With the drip bottle in place and Paul Wilson tightly strapped to the trolley, the drip was set to flow faster into his body.

"No…Noooo." Within minutes, Paul Wilson's screams drifted away as he fell into a permanent sleep.

Chapter Twenty

Isobel Cooper put herself in a position where she could keep her eye on Doctor Bijarani. The doctor, for the time being, was safe, surrounded by his brothers, supporters, and benefactors. She scanned the room, making sure that her target was visible at all times, as she waited for the moment to move in. This would be a difficult mission, with over four hundred people in the conference room. If she moved too soon, trying to reach Doctor Bijarani through the crowd, it would create mayhem. Being too late wasn't an option either.

Isobel found the burka disguise uncomfortable, lacking the freedom she would need to move quickly. In the stifling heat of the room, she found the garment almost suffocating.

And then she saw *him* as *he* watched the doctor. Silently, she approached the smartly dressed, black-suited figure.

But Hosani Islamabad felt the slight breeze of her burka as she crept closer to him. He turned to face her.

Isobel backed away from him, towards the doorway leading to the kitchen. She had to draw him away from the crowd to somewhere she could confront the Hassassini. He looked around the room before following her.

She led him into a corridor where the Hassassini quickly pulled a knife from his jacket pocket and flicked it open. As he lunged at the girl, she immediately snapped the blade from his hand with a well-placed punch to his wrist, sending it clattering along the empty corridor.

The Hassassini lunged at the girl. She parried his blows at her face and body, trying to fend him off. Her training worked for several minutes, but she stood little chance of putting her combat training into full use, while wearing the cumbersome burka. For a few moments, she held her own against a stronger and freer adversary.

Eventually, he took hold of the loose garment and whipped the girl around. With her back against him; he snapped her neck in one swift movement. Isobel Cooper fell to the floor.

Grabbing her legs, the assailant dragged her through the nearest door and into the kitchen lobby.

He straightened and brushed himself down. Now he had to get to his target before the speeches started. The confrontation had cost him valuable time. It was an unexpected intrusion, perfectly handled.

Chapter Twenty-One

The conference hall was full, with the rumble of hundreds of voices talking in unison. Friday prayers finished moments ago, and now refreshments were being taken before the main event of the evening.

The guest speaker, Doctor Mohamed Bijarani, mingled with prominent members of leading imams and invited dignitaries from other religions, who came to hear his pleas for peace and reconciliation. The doctor was due to speak at an awards ceremony to be given on his behalf and to be presented with a scroll for his contribution to peace.

Doctor Mohamed Bijarani spent the last six years of his life travelling the world in an attempt to convince his people to end the relentless cycle of terrorism and killing everywhere. His main mission in life was to end radicalisation and to stop the young from being drawn into its clutches.

Over the years, he had met with governments of many countries, encouraging them to create a dialogue with the warring factions, and persuading them to refuse sanctuary in those evil bands. He preached that terrorism was the work of a few misguided people and not the ideals of many. He constantly visited mosques, temples and churches and met leaders of all faiths, lecturing on the war against terrorism. All with the same message…peace. Today he was here in Glasgow to continue his message.

As Bannister and Pullman entered the conference room, they did not know who they were looking for at first. As they scanned over the heads of over four hundred people, Malcolm had the advantage of his six-foot four height and towered over most of the crowd in the room.

In the centre of the room, he noticed more activity than anywhere else. He and Pullman approached the group and the small man at the hub of all the attention.

"Doctor Bijarani?" asked Bob Pullman.

"Yes?" the doctor replied in a voice that was quiet, calm, and almost angelic.

Bannister liked the little man immediately. Doctor Bijarani was a small man, about five foot two, and very slim. He was dressed from top to bottom in a pale cream suit, with an open-neck white shirt. Instead of shoes, he wore sandals on his feet without socks. Bob Pullman likened him to a modern-day Mahatma Gandhi. A quiet man with an aura of gentleness about him.

"Doctor Bijarani. My name is detective Malcolm Bannister, and this is my colleague, detective Bob Pullman." Both men showed their warrant cards to the doctor. "Would you care to come with us, please?" Banister said quietly, almost in a whisper.

"Am I under arrest?" asked the doctor, surprised.

"On the contrary, sir," replied Bannister.

THE HASSASSINI

"However, if you value your life, it would be best if you came with us, sir. Try not to attract too much attention to yourself and us. Please come with us."

"But…but I have a speech to deliver," he stammered, "as you know, I am trying to stop young men and women becoming radicalised into evil groups who do not teach the true teachings of Islam, but use Islam as a means and excuse to create havoc and violence worldwide."

"We are well aware of your good work, sir. However, we also know that if you make the speech, you may not leave this building alive," Bannister said.

"What!" exclaimed the shocked doctor. "My friends. I feel perfectly safe here. I am surrounded by my friends and brothers who will protect me."

"Not everyone in this room thinks of you as their brother." Bannister was becoming aware the doctor assumed no harm would come to him and sighed.

Pullman reached into his jacket pocket and

pulled out a folded sheet of paper. Looking around the room while keeping the paper low and close to his body, he whispered to the doctor, "When I show you this, Doctor Bijarani, try not to appear surprised." Unfolding the paper, he showed it to the doctor.

Doctor Bijarani's eyes widened, and he opened his mouth to gasp, but checked himself in time.

"Do you know what this is, sir?"

The doctor hesitated for a moment before answering, "Yes, I recognise this evil symbol," he sighed. "These are some of the very people I am fighting against."

"What does this symbol mean, Doctor?" Pullman asked.

Doctor Bijarani took a deep breath before replying. "It is an assassination creed within our community. Its tentacles reach around the globe. An evil organisation which targets specific individuals…like me, people who believe in the true teachings of Islam." He paused to reflect on

THE HASSASSINI

what he was saying. "These Hassassini, on the other hand, use the holy name of Islam to kill us, the peacemakers, to create violence and mayhem to force others to do their will. They believe that followers of Islam will one day rule the world."

"And you don't, sir?" Asked Pullman.

He looked down at his open hands in sadness. "No. It will not happen. Through time immemorial, many religions tried to live in harmony. None succeeded." Glancing up at the two faces in front of him, he added, "Even in your own Christian community, between Catholics and Protestants, there are great divides. It has never worked in thousands of years. The best we can ever hope for is to live in peace with one another… even Gandhi tried and failed to unite Hindus and Sikhs in his own country."

Bannister nodded solemnly. It was well known that Doctor Bijarani's radical thinking created many enemies as well as friends. "Your work is admirable, sir, but you need to watch your back. These people, The Hassassini, are violent to the extreme, as you rightly said. We have seen their evil first hand in the past few days, doctor." He pondered for a moment. "Do you have protection, doctor?"

"By that, do you mean do I have bodyguards? Then no. I am a man of peace, and I am surrounded by friends." He waved his arms at the throng of followers around him. "It is unlikely that an assassin would reach me. These brothers are my protection."

"Mahatma Ghandi was a man of peace. He too was surrounded by thousands of friends, and look what happened to him!" replied Malcolm Bannister.

"I take your point, sir, and I thank you for your concern," Mohamed Bijarani smiled, bowing slightly.

"In that case, doctor, at least allow us to provide some security around the room for you until you complete your speech."

Doctor Mohamed Bijarani nodded his agreement, shook hands with the two men, and returned to join his benefactors.

Chapter Twenty-Two

The two partners mingled with the crowd, hoping their experienced eyes would spot something which detectives were supposed to see, which members of the public don't. They separated, with Pullman casually walking around the room, opening and closing doors, making sure no one was hiding. Meanwhile, Bannister kept a close eye on the people nearest to the doctor by using his six foot four height advantage to scan over the heads of most of the crowd in the room.

Bannister's mobile rang. Quickly, he slapped it to his ear. "Malc," Pullman said, "get the fuck over here quick, I'm in the north lobby leading to the kitchens."

Bannister arrived to see Pullman kneeling over

a body. The girl lay crumpled in a heap. Her eyes, wide open in death, stared at the ceiling, her neck twisted and broken.

"Who is she? Do we know?" Bannister asked.

"From the pic we had in the car. It's our missing female, Isobel Cooper: I remember her face. Damn!" replied Pullman in a saddened voice. "Look at her left shoulder." He pointed to where a piece of her burka which was torn in the struggle.

Bannister looked closely at the tattoo, but the Arabic word اغتيال *'assassin.'* was not there!

"Oh, my God. *Whichever one you are,*" shouted Bannister. "She was *not* the assassin."

"I don't believe it!" Pullman Exclaimed. "Are you sure?"

"Yes. That tattoo is a fake!" With a handkerchief, Bannister moistened it. Then gently running it over part of the tattoo. He found some of the colour had rubbed on to the white handkerchief. "It is a simple transfer."

"Call it in Bob. Get Constable Mahmood in here to stand guard over the body until forensics gets here."

"Malcolm, if she's not the assassin, then who killed her, and why?"

"Maybe she was tailing the assis…Oh shit, the doctor!" Bannister shot out of the lobby, followed by his partner. With Pullman unholstering his Glock on the move, he pushed his way into the crowd, who were still unaware of the murder. They shoved their way to where they last saw Doctor Bijarani.

"He's okay," called Pullman, as he watched the doctor scratch at his right leg, then stood up again, surrounded by his audience.

They returned to the body of Isobel Cooper, to await the arrival of the forensic team. "Seal off the hotel and announce no one is to enter or leave," Bannister ordered.

THE HASSASSINI

As they broadcasted announcement over the speaker on the podium, there were angry exchanges with some of the crowd, as a dozen policemen surrounded the hotel room. Bannister would make an official statement once everyone had settled.

As they attended the body of Isobel Cooper, someone in the crowd screamed. Bannister rushed back into the room and pushed through the panicking crowd to see Doctor Bijarani lying on the floor. The cream suited doctor lay on the ground clutching his left leg…he was dead. A tiny trickle of blood stained the trouser leg.

Like Matamata Gandhi, Doctor Mohamed Bijarani was surrounded by his so-called *friends* when he died.

Chapter Twenty-Three

Three days later, they found the body of Paul Wilson, still strapped to the trolley in a strip of waste ground on the outskirts of the city. The drip bottle was still in place, but empty. Mercifully, he had not been tortured or mutilated, but simply put to sleep by the drip overdose.

Chapter Twenty-Four

A week after the assassination of Doctor Mohamed Bijarani, Superintendent Billy Monkhouse summoned Bannister and Pullman into his office. In front of them, their boss stood resplendently adorned in his full dress uniform, complete with white gloves, with his medals and his decorations proudly pinioned to his left shoulder. "I would like you both to come with me, please."

    Billy Monkhouse led the two colleagues down to his official car, a stunning black BMX X5, with a policewoman driver waiting for them. As they sat in the car, Monkhouse announced. "I am retiring from the force as of today…now in fact. I have cleared my office, and this car will take me straight home after the funeral."

"Funeral?" commented a surprised Bannister. "Who is being buried?"

As the car drove into the cemetery, Bannister looked ahead at the open grave. It was the grave of Billy Monkhouse's wife. He was last here eight years ago as a pallbearer when they buried Angela Monkhouse, after she succumbed after a short and sudden fight with cancer. At the time, it broke Billy Monkhouse's heart. It was the first and only time Bannister saw his boss cry.

"Sir, who are we burying?" asked Pullman.

He raised his head and with tears coursing down his face, replied. "My daughter!"

Bannister and Pullman looked at each other. "Did we know your daughter, sir?"

"No, but you have both seen her." Tears formed in his eyes, which he wiped away with a handkerchief taken from his pocket. "Isobel Cooper was my daughter. That is why I asked you to…to…to put a watch on her on the night the assassin was killed in her flat." He stifled a sob.

"Shit!" swore Bannister.

"I understand your frustration, detective."

"I very much doubt that, *sir*," Bannister fumed angrily.

Pullman said, "She pulverised the guy, Billy!"

"No, she didn't; she wasn't there. The guy who ran was an undercover police decoy, I am ashamed to say. He killed the assassin in self-defence." Monkhouse bowed his head. "I sent Isobel somewhere else that night. We were warned that she'd been rumbled, and it was true. The guy came to eliminate her, so we had to get her away. But I needed someone to be in the flat to draw the assassin. He was one of the Hassassini.

"Why destroy his face?" Bannister asked.

"We didn't. Someone else must have come to the flat later to make him unrecognisable."

"And at the conference?" asked Pullman

"When we finally found out the identity of the real assassin, Isobel was there to confront him, disguised as an Arab woman, complete with the burka. She was a well-trained undercover police woman and an expert martial arts fighter. I can only assume that when she confronted the assassin, he proved to be too powerful for her..." Monkhouse hesitated. "...and she lost her life." Tears fell freely from the superintendent's eyes.

"The tattoo on her shoulder differed from the others. The word 'assassin' was missing," said Bannister.

"A fake, a henna drawing, which washes off."

Anger finally took hold of Bannister. "We could have saved your daughter, Monkhouse, if you had been more upfront and trusted us. Trusted *me*... after these thirty years together. You stupid fool."

"I know…I know that now!"

"You sacrificed Isobel Cooper, your own daughter!" Malcolm Bannister fumed, "and after all that, the Hassassini bastard got away."

Bannister leaned forward with his face buried in his hands, "There are times when I hate this fucking job," he hollered, looking at his former boss, "and the people in it…stop the fucking car!" Malcolm Bannister opened the door, slammed it shut, and walked off in the opposite direction.

Chapter Twenty-Five

Hosani Isamabad sat back as the thrust of the A380 United Arab Airway's four Rolls-Royce engines forced themselves into the clear blue sky, and up to its cruising height of thirty-six thousand feet. He was a man satisfied. His mission was successful, and his bank balance had increased significantly.

It was unfortunate he eliminated a fellow assassin at the girl's flat and not the girl. They would not recognise the dead Hassassini after he hammered his face into a bloody pulp. The undercover bitch Isobel Cooper had been a thorn in the flesh since she discovered 'The Hassassini Creed.' But she became useful by turning up at the conference. Cooper put up a good fight, but she

THE HASSASSINI

made a mistake, and he took advantage of it.

The finding of her body by the two cops created the distraction he needed to put the needle into the doctor's thigh. The delaying effect of the poison would take five to ten minutes to kill him. At first, it would appear that he had a heart attack. It gave the Hassassini enough time to leave the building quietly, to the waiting car outside the conference hall which would speed him to the airport.

With the aircraft settled into its cruising height, the Hassassini relaxed into a quiet slumber. The beautiful hostess looked down at the handsome 'businessman'. "Can I get you something, sir?" she asked.

"Easir aprcot min fadlik." *'Apricot juice, please',* he said to the smiling air hostess leaning over him as he read her name on the gold badge on her white blouse; Alsama. A few moments later, Alsama returned with his refreshment. Hosani Isamabad slipped her a large tip with a note, suggesting that they meet when she was free.

She smiled sweetly, but said nothing

Seven hours later, as the A380 landed at King Khalid International Airport in Riyadh.

The beautiful Hassassini, Alsama Moghadam, picked up the empty glass at the feet of Hosani Isamabad. Lifting his limp arm hanging by his side, she put it on his lap, closed his wide-open dead eyes, and called the captain.

"Sir, we have a passenger who may have had a heart attack on seat twenty-four in first class."

The pilot nodded and smiled as he tapped his left shoulder… *The Hassassini are everywhere.*

النهاية

The end

Glasgow in Scotland and London, England, in search of the four diamonds called… 'Water'…'Fire'…'Earth'…'Air.'

Available on Amazon

Russell Glashan

Also on Amazon is the following historical thriller

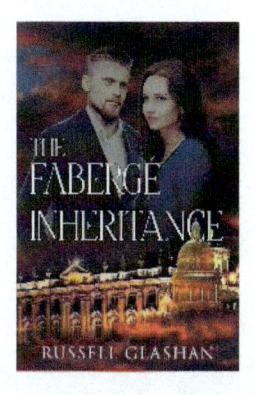

In the year 1894, Peter Carl Fabergé finds his long lost brother, dead. Amidst the sorrow, he adopts his new found nephew, Anatoli and decides to bring him into the illustrious Fabergé workshop. Here, Anatoli's talent flourishes. After a heated confrontation, Anatoli storms out, leaving behind a final, cursed piece, a brooch—a piece imbued with his rage and sorrow.

Fast forward to the present day, this enigmatic artifact reemerges at a high-profile auction, capturing the attention of Charles, the future Lord Buckworth, and Natalia, a dedicated fine arts investigator. Together, they embark on a journey to uncover the origins and hidden secrets of Anatoli's last creation.

Available on Amazon

Russell Glashan

Printed in Great Britain
by Amazon